Collected Stories

Anne Harlan

ISBN
979-8-218-05713-8

ANNA AND THE PRIEST

It was only revealed to me in the last years of her life. The apparent romance of her grandmother with the family friend, a young priest who was her age. How long it continued will never be known.

Her mother hinted at it and was accused of being delusional. But years later the granddaughter witnessed an exchange between the two when entering a room without knocking.

The grandmother was in her chemise and the priest was pinching her cheek playfully. Upon discovery, she walked over and handed the girl of bit of cash.

Neither shocked nor dismayed the girl said she withdrew from the doorway and never told anyone. She thought of her mother's insinuations.

She remembered passing her grandfather just minutes before she entered the room. He was walking, pacing really, the corridor. He had a certain twinkle in his eyes.

On reflection years later, the girl says her devout grandfather felt he was assured a place in heaven.

WHY

She had small hands, dainty hands; and that was not the only remarkable feature about her. The fingernails on her left hand, the little finger and the ring finger were nubs. Apparently, rather than chew all her nails, she would concentrate on just these two fingers of her left hand.

I wanted her to take me into her confidence. Why these two fingers? Is this a conscious move or merely a harmless pastime?

Setting in motion the plan to gain her confidence began. She is a walker so I asked to join her. She declined as she prefers to walk alone and listen to music. There has to be another way to stimulate a budding friendship.

Why do I pursue this I ask myself. It is simply because I want to know; I want to know why because subconscious or not there is a reason for the two shortened nails.

As fate would have it, I regularly drive past the area where she walks. It was rainy and I asked her if she wanted a lift. That began our friendship.

Five years have passed and I am now her confidante. I learned the story of the abbreviated nails and will impart it to you.

It was a love story, a story of sadness and retaliation. A story where there is no good guy, there is no bad guy, just youth and young hearts easily led astray. Not astray for lack of love but an ignorance of love. Tragic and sad, just plain sad.

They need no names, nor description. Know only that they met at 16 in high school. A mutual attraction, they would talk on the phone for hours in the evening. She told him she hoped she died first because she did not want to go through life without him. It was not to be, he died at the age of 21. It was in the month of September, a day bright with sunshine.

She went on for years without him. Days would pass and she would not think of him. The remorse of parting subsided. She enjoyed life for the most part. Their parting consisted of him telling her if anything ever happened to him it was her fault. It was his final chess-like move to tattoo himself on her brain forever.

Now she visits his grave to deposit in the soil her two fingernails from her left hand. A small penance she realizes as he joined the Marines because she wanted to see other people. His revenge was sacrificing his life to an unpopular war which was never won.

WHO KNOWS WHERE THE MIND GOES

Her reveries had not really changed much over the years. Now at 80, she thought her dreams would come to fruition.

His name was Johnny McKenna and she met him during the Second World War. A brief affair, probably one among countless others that occurred during this terrible time.

She was married and remained so after the war. Few knew of this infidelity, and she was fearful to ever mention this passing romance.

Days passed slowly and the weeks passed quickly. She lost her beloved husband to an early death. After this loss, she survived only for her daughter to whom after many years she told of her affair with Johnny McKenna.

Where did her mind go during those many years? Then at 80, she seemed to be more lively and even enthusiastic at times.

The years had left her with unstable legs that required walking with a cane, Yet at 80 she began to try to get about without assistance, falling but without injury.

This transformation was explained as she then related her affair to me. Johnny had told her he would look her up when they turned 80. She had clung to that since 1968 the year her husband died. The husband she chose over Johnny McKenna.

WENDY, WHAT WENT WRONG?

Met her in her 50th year, had remembered
her as having a housekeeping position in the office
building. The work there was specific to special
needs and she seemed to be one of those. No
matter, she was employed.

She wore bracelets, many bracelets that laced
up her arm colorfully. Her hair, white, was butch
cut though she seemed totally asexual. She liked to
talk.

Somehow she managed to talk herself into a
better position with an office next to mine. She
would often stop to chat mostly about her life, her
earlier life. She told me she sold her father's pain
pills to local druggies.

Finally her erratic behavior and outlandish
stories landed her back in housekeeping, then she
became unemployed due to mental issues. She
could be spotted often in the "dirty" mall exchanging
stories with local misfits.

Last word, she lives in a home for the elderly
and her erratic behavior is being dealt with. She has
a condition, it is explained.

JUST WALK ON BY

He watched for her from his second story bedroom window. The house, off Artillery Blvd. faced the walking loop across from his house.

It did not go unnoticed to her that no matter the time of day she went, he was there walking the loop as well. They always walked in opposite directions.

Only once was there an exchange of words as he blurted "watch it" at her as, eyes downcast, she nearly collided with him.

He was initially told of her presence in the park by his four buddies that walked the loop daily. They had spotted her and claiming "you gotta see her" had aroused his curiosity. And now, he looks for her and despite his better judgement he walked the loop just to pass her and perhaps have eye contact.

Then one morning, as they were approaching one another, a friend of his called out to him "what are you doing here again?" Aghast, he barely answered his friend, and head bowed, he quickly passed her.

She reached her car as he ran by, which was a pace she had never seen from him before, She briefly wondered if this had to do with her.

She chose another park in which to spend her walking time. He never even knew her name.

THE WAITER

There he was, head held high as he strolled across the parking lot into the restaurant that had employed him for nearly a year. He wore a black tee shirt with I LOVE MY JOB emblazoned across the back with a bright red heart accentuating the sentiment.

He is a busboy, hoping to become a waiter within the next few days. He liked the clink of the dishes as he collects them from the newly abandoned tables, but he longed for the better paying waiter's job.

The day was here finally and his replacement greeted him as they both entered the door. They had arrived promptly, ready to work.

After the late afternoon prep for the dinner hour with silverware and napkins made ready for the recently cleaned tables, he awaited the first guests.

As the guests began arriving he found the 4 tables assigned to him filled quickly. He greeted them at the table, placing the menus in front of them. As the family of five arrived first he saw to them quickly. It was a mother, father and three young children. He took the drink orders saying he would return soon for the food orders.

Another table at the next booth was a table of young men. They also were in his section. He gave them a nod of the head and proceeded to the beverages.

The family placed their food orders as the children entertained themselves with the puzzle placemats set on the table. It was a large order.

The table of young men grumbled that he had not taken their orders yet. As he heard his number, number one called out, he hurried to retrieve the food order.

The tray was heavy and awkward for him to carry. As he approached the family, passing the young men again, one called out to him, "hey, number one, and extended his foot tripping the poor waiter. Food and waiter came crashing to the floor much to the horror of all the observers.

In confusion and embarrassment he rose and ran out of the front door of the restaurant, promising himself, he would never wait tables again or interact with the public. He became a dog walker.

DÉJÀ VU

I am reincarnated. We are all reincarnated. My family of 5 including our pets have been here before. The concept is not new. Throughout time individuals have questioned their reality and their very existence.

Within the family we are aware of this phenomenon. We know who we were previously. What is so unusual is that we were each well-known.

As the Mother I watch over the family and attempt to find some levity in our lives. Ironically, I was Virginia Woolf in a past life. Being a suicide, I have a different approach to life as well as with my family. I took my life because of severe depression. Now with my family I attempt to be cheerful, but this facade can be overwhelming.

Now, let us begin with the family members individually. Aside from me, there is my husband, my three children and our dog and an incidental snake. Two boys and a girl (which can be a trial in itself), make up the members of the household. So, there we are for this introduction.

Have I learned something from my past lives? Do I really know how many times I have returned? The other lives have faded from memory. Only occasionally do I get a glimpse of what I have already seen. Fortunately, I don't remember all of the pain that can go along with being a living creature. This pain, however, can be a reminder, a

13

call from past lives. As we all know, life is hard, even our dog Hamlet has bad days.

Now to my husband Jack. In his past the most memorable person of note that he can remember is Jean-Jacques Rousseau. It seems Jack has carried some of that philosophical approach to life into this current time.

Our sons, Thomas and Phillip, have the ages of 12 and 10 respectively. Thomas in the past was Ingmar Bergman while Phillip was the actor James Cagney. An odd pairing of brothers. One once a director and the other an actor of note. As brothers will do, they have disagreements, mostly because Thomas tries to tell Phillip what to do.

And finally, there is our daughter, Celeste. Celeste, a girl of 14, was Cleopatra and curiously enough she is fond of snakes, in fact she has a pet snake. When she is acting up we always tell her not to make an asp of herself.

Naturally, it is difficult to determine who our dog and the snake were before, but we do have our suppositions. Jack and I think the snake was a politician but when we attempt to delve further he slithers away under the rock in his terrarium. We think that Hamlet was William Shakespeare. No surprise there really. He does seem to bark a lot; his way of being prolific, I suppose. And in character, he never seems to know whether he wants to go out or stay inside. In other words, to pee or not to pee.

The evening meal is always interesting. The dog stays in his little doghouse during that time. All we have to say is go to Stratford-upon-Avon. Preparation of the meal usually falls on me. Celeste has no interest in the kitchen and generally will not lift a finger to assist. Our conversations at the table are diverse. Jack, philosophizes, Thomas and I are morose. Celeste languishes over the meal and rarely speaks. Phillip is usually ready for confrontation that can result in a pugilistic scene. But it must be noted that Phillip can really dance well when he puts his mind to it, but why he whistles Yankee Doodle Dandy is beyond me.

We are currently trying to determine where we can vacation together as a family. My aversion to water is definitely a drawback; yet in accordance with this, Celeste prefers the desert. Thomas does not care where we go because life is short and of little consequence. Phillip wants to climb a mountain so he can feel on top of the world. And Jack will go anywhere that includes enjoying nature.

So our little assembly must come to a decision about the projected vacation. At last we decide to visit Bruges, Belgium and have chosen our accommodations. We know it is out of the question for Thomas and Phillip to share a room, Jack in his agreeable fashion is willing for me to have a room of my own. Now it is Celeste's turn not to care where we go. Thomas has already stated that he must be able to bring his chessboard. And of course Phillip is up for the chess challenge.

As we live in a small town in Ohio, this vacation will be monumental in all of our lives. I am a bit apprehensive of going such a distance, but I will rely on the calm temperament of Jack. He has always managed to deflect my fears.

Our knowledge of each other's past lives does not limit us as we lived in different times. In fact, we know little of one another's stories. We think it best to move forward and not dwell on the past events which were notable in each life. To me, it is ironic that Celeste and I, the two females in the family, both took their own lives. We avoid this topic. Besides, I don't think Celeste is aware of her final days. However, she did name her snake Julius.

It cannot be confirmed that glimpses of past events we experience actually occurred. But the overwhelming feeling of having done something before, something familiar, persists. So often it goes unsaid, as we have accepted that we do indeed return. Some of us have the ability to see forms of those that hover about. These are souls that have not entered another body yet. Jack and I believe that we continue to return until we get it right. Right with who you ask? We don't know. Can it be an exemplary life that when we pass over our souls become light, pure energy, that dissipates? Then there is nothing but peace and then nothingness.

It is like before we are born-no sentient memory.

But I digress. It is when this feeling overcomes me that I am compelled to talk of matters that defy explanation. Yet I always try to understand and convey our feelings of life beyond the grave. There are souls not at rest-could it be a form of purgatory? I don't know. I don't think these souls find peace through prayer although I have been told that any fervent wish is a prayer. The thought of praying to a superior being is foolish to Jack and me as well. I feel the children are too young to wrestle with these matters of the soul.

So the trip is planned. We will drive to Cincinnati and take a jet to Brussels, Belgium and then rent a car and drive to Bruges. We are all excited now about our journey to parts unknown. We have also done our research about this ancient city. Bruges is the capital of West Flanders in northwest Belgium. It is distinguished by its canals, cobbled streets, and medieval buildings. Much of the history dates back to the 11th century; however, much emphasis has been given to the 14th century. While there, we want to visit the Historium which lets the visitor step back in time. It will tell us the story of the 14th century painter Jan Van Eyck. Van Eyck moved to Bruges in 1429 where he lived until his death in 1441. Known as an Early Netherlandish painter, he is considered one of the most significant representatives of Early Northern Renaissance art. It is fascinating to know that he is one of the first painters to sign his work. The entire family, excluding the pets, feel drawn to this city with its rich history. The flight was uneventful and we slept through the short night to awaken to early morning in Brussels. My constant question is how many times have we returned? Is it cyclical? Or are there certain souls that never return? Their transgressions are so deep, so terrible that they are doomed to wander in a sphere unknown to many.

As we take to the autoroute, we are all enjoying the scenery. The verdure and beauty of the region is truly mesmerizing. Even the children seem to be enchanted by their surroundings. The hour and 15 minute drive from Brussels to Bruges was very pleasant. The windmills are slowly turning like our minds turning with reflections.

We arrive in the afternoon and find our hotel after parking at the train station. This little town is

best seen by foot. The hotel met with our
expectations and breakfast was included in the price.
We all decided to stay awake until evening to stave
off jetlag. Our perambulations in the town will begin
slowly as we are still recovering from the long flight
followed by the drive with the automobile we rented
at the airport.

Odd, how it all seems familiar, from the little
cobbled streets to the buildings and the canals that
wend their way through the town. We are delighted
that we made this choice of vacation. And we are
impatient to see the Historium and other places of
interest. The short walk we took in the park near the
train station was enough for the day. We returned to
the hotel and had dinner then to bed.

We awoke to a foggy, rainy day; however, this
did not deter us. We headed for the Historium.
There we found that there is a film to be shown
about Jan Van Eyck and his painting of the Virgin
and Child commissioned by Canon van der Paele as
an altar piece. It took Van Eyck 2 years to complete
the painting. He began in 1434 and finished in 1436.
We are told that the tour will evoke sights, smells,
and sounds in a Proustian fashion.

As the tour begins, we enter the first room
which tells the story of Jacob an apprentice to Van
Eyck. He is to seek out the woman, Anna, who will
sit for the painting. We are all confused by the sights
and sounds and smells of the past. Our son Thomas
is fascinated by the role of the apprentice. He says
there is something so familiar about the journey that
Jacob takes to seek out Anna.

Enroute, Jacob is accosted by thieves that try
to steal his rosary which was given to him by his

mother. During this scene Thomas becomes agitated and wishes to leave, to end the tour. We persuade him to stay and continue to the next room and next scene in the story of the painting. During the scuffle Jacob gets only a brief glimpse of Anna. She has disappeared into the crowd at the dock.

Now it is Celeste's turn to find a connection, this one to Anna. She says she has felt the fear of the young woman and finds that this is an eerie moment of realization. A realization that brings her to the conclusion that this is more than empathy.

The Canon that appears in the painting seems to strike a chord with my husband, Jack. How ironic that he would be able to relate to someone with a religious background. As Rousseau, he believed the religion of man to be informal and unorganized, centering on morality and the worship of God.

Unfortunately, Phillip feels a tie with the mugger that attempts to steal the amber rosary from Jacob. Again there are altercations with Thomas.

As the drama unfolds, it is revealed that Jacob's rosary was sold to a kind woman who saw Jacob's misery and pitied him. She returns the rosary to him.

The time has now come to see Van Eyck's workshop. As I watch, I realize that it is the person to which I can strongly identify as having been attached to him in another life.

So now it is apparent that in another life we were the same people that are portrayed in the film we have been watching at the Historium in Bruges, Belgium. Astonishing to think that we were once connected in the 14th century in this same town.

19

These connections unite us with the strong bonds to the past.

How can this be I ask myself. It is an impossibility yet it has happened. Our past lives have come together to present us with this impossibility. We all lived in the same time period and had encounters with one another,

As we leave the Historium, we keep silent. The emotions felt in our souls has not given us peace, merely an astounding sense of knowing.

I will end my story here. We believe we have returned many times but rarely have we been well-known individuals. It is very rare for a soul to realize that there is or can be a shared past. I do not wish to come back again; I can only hope my life will truly end this time with the release of my soul to an astral plane unknown, unimaginable, solely a place of peace.

UNFAITHFUL

As a young girl she was told "men are only after one thing," In her innocence she wondered—what?

Now as an adult and through the years, she has grown wiser. This wisdom grows out of experience and wisdom can sometimes be a cruel teacher.

It was not just one, but several of her past lovers who were now married expected an affair with her. They did not respect her unwillingness to become involved with them. This was from a moral sense of responsibility and self-protection along with self-respect. For her, an affair with a married man was out of the question.

She sometimes told herself, it is not their fault, it is their innate need to procreate. This however, ignores the psychological implications.

So when her married former lover with a wife and children told her " I am glad you have cats" it made her cry as a family was never an option for her.

TIL THE END

I said I do, but I didn't. I said , I know, but I didn't. I said I would, but I didn't.

A good opener for anyone non? It raises a plethora of questions. One demands, but why didn't you? It is not time for self-reproach. Those times will always pass. Let go, let yourself breathe. It is not good to look inside yourself too long. Truer words were never spoken.

RIP to those that looked inside—perhaps too long.

THE MAGIC OF THE THRIFT SHOP

She loved to indulge in thrift shopping. Found it quite an adventure. She began this quest years before it became so in vogue. She avoided the consignment shops and remained with the shops that depended solely on donations.

After a successful morning of shopping, she marveled that she returned home with glasses, baskets, plates, and was able to find some apparel still unworn with the tags on it, donated by someone that had made a hasty purchase.

Occasionally, she would intentionally purchase a shirt or blouse that had been worn by someone else. She liked the idea that someone else had worn this article of clothing.
She felt she drew their energy to herself and reveled in the very idea of this. Although at times, she feared the possibility of negative, depressive energy.

One rainy day, she dashed in for a quick look around. She had already decided to get something someone else had worn. She made her selection; it was a blouse. A simple blouse, white, with a round collar. It was the only item she bought.

Leaving the store, she found it had already begun to grow dark on this cold, wintry day. She was anxious to see how the blouse looked as she did not take time to try it on,

As she regarded herself in the mirror, she liked the reflection. The blouse fit well. Suddenly an inexplicable lethargy overcame her. She sank to the floor, striking her head on the nearby vanity. Her final, dying thought was I finally got the black magic.

THIS OLD HOUSE

How many times has he turned the key in the lock of the door? How many times has he entered the darkening room with the darker curtains? He regards the room dispassionately. It is only after spending some time there that the memories begin to invade his consciousness.

Entering the foyer he wonders how often he has bent into the front door in order to turn the lock. He looks out onto the screened-in front porch that has remained the same for over 90 years, The tall hemlocks planted by his great-grandmother provide privacy.

Standing in front of the refrigerator in the basement, he recalls the many popsicles sought on hot summer days in a similar refrigerator 60 years ago.

As he climbs the stairs from the basement to the first floor, he recalls the stories of his great-grandfather's fall. The fall down the stairs that led to his death.

Ascending the stairs to the second floor of the house, he surveys the large room that was once his; the one he shared with his older brother.

Now the house is to be sold. A house his family has owned and occupied for 92 years.

Again he thinks of the prospect dispassionately. It is not a matter of letting go. He did that when he went out the door at the age of 18. The times shared in the house will always be part of him. It formed him, formed many of the ways in which he reacts to events in his life.

As he leaves the house for the last time, peace settles over him. There is no attachment, no lasting somber memory. The gate closes slowly behind him.

THE TREE

It was a beautiful, fragrant Japanese magnolia that was planted by the house's new occupants. The year was 1929.

The tree flourished and grew. After several years, when spring arrived the tree began unfolding its pink blossoms. A sudden cold snap in early spring could mean no blooms for the season. This was harshly disappointing for not only the house's owners but the neighbors as well.

The tree was admired and cared for by the descendants of the original gardener who planted the tree. This spanned 92 years.

It was a popular tree to climb for the middle child living there during the 60s. The eleven-year-old could sit comfortably in the tree for hours. She delighted in summer when the windows were open wide. She could hear the doorbell ring from it's place on the wall in the kitchen. Her hiding place did not last long as a family member would search for her there in the tree when visitors came to call.

On those spring days, the tree's beauty and fragrance caused passersby to stop take a photo or ask the species of this deciduous tree.

Years passed and the eleven-year-old became a 25 year old who had long abandoned the tree climbing activities. Though from time to time, she would turn a wistful gaze to the tree.

Time passed and so did the family members. There was just one occupant left. It was decided the house would be sold. The process proceeded quickly and a new home was found—a condominium.

The tree took no notice of the change within the house. It merely stood proud and majestic.

The former home's owner liked to drive past and see the work being done remodeling the house. Early spring came and drew the house's seller back to see the tree. It was dead.

Irony, coincidence, whatever your point of view.

THE AUCTION

It was his idea, his brain child. Why not auction off something that belonged to a dead rock star. An article of clothing or shoes. Yes, he knew people would jump at the chance to wear a pair of high-heeled shoes worn by Prince. Then how about a feather boa worn by Janis Joplin or Jim Morrison's shirt torn by fans? And to think the possibility of owning a headband worn by Jimi Hendrix. Any of these items would bring in a good amount. Not that he needed the money, it was just a project he wanted to pursue.

Yes, this idea was going to work. He set about researching contacts, sent out feelers to people that knew people. His passion to auction these collected items began on November 24,1991 when Freddie Mercury drew his last breath. The auctioneer just wanted to be associated with these names of rock history both past and present. Then in 1994 Kurt Cobain took his own life.

He thought enough, I have slowly accumulated every article I thought would be of interest to those that wanted to attend a "rock auction." Time passed but he still had not put his plan into motion.

Then finally, in 2016 he decided to sell. The auction house was filled with those that were curious and those that were devoted fans of the various rock stars. It was the death of Prince that was the motivating factor for the auctioneer.

Things were moving along as the throng of people took their seats. He began the auction by breaking into his Elvis impersonation offering the first item. It was the cape worn by Elvis when he met President Nixon. Next was the feather boa Janis Joplin wore in her first concert with The Brothers on June 4, 1966 at the Avalon Ballroom in San Francisco.

The evening went on with bids on the torn shirt Morrison left behind when he left for France. His death July 3, 1971, in Paris was a shock to rockers in all nations.

As Freddie Mercury's Queen concerts were called "a fashion show" the jumpsuit he wore drew high dollars as it was the one he wore to his final concert in Knebworth Park Festival in 1986 UK.

When it came to a pair of shoes that reportedly Michael Jackson moonwalked in, the house shook with enthusiasm and bids.

The evening was growing tiresome for him and he decided to close with eyeglasses of two performers that died decades apart. He first put on a pair of glasses worn by the late Buddy Holly which also went for a remarkable price. Then for the closing he chose the only suicide—Kurt Cobain. He slowly placed the aviator sunglasses on his face. The room grew dark despite the bright lights.

Suddenly his face filled with a quiet resolve. As a precaution and unsure what to expect from the crowd, he had placed a pistol inside one of the small shelves of the auctioneer podium. He withdrew the pistol and turning his head upright, chin towards the ceiling he placed the barrel beneath his chin and pulled the trigger.

Why? The evening had been a success. Why? Had he accomplished what he had set out to do or did Kurt invade his consciousness with his despair? The answer will never be known.

STANDING ON THE CORNER

Bleak is my name, Victor Bleak and bleak are my prospects. You see I am homeless. I panhandle. I ask for handouts because I can no longer stand the pressures of trying to make a living at a job.

How many people pass me on a daily basis? I have no idea though sometimes I notice the repeats.

Yes, I dropped out. I left family and friends behind as I could no longer face them as the failure that I am.

Standing on the corner, I hold my little sign pleading for sympathy and a monetary boost to my self-esteem. I question myself. Am I a sympathetic creature only asking for some help? Does my face speak volumes about my life? Who even looks at my face?

Yes, the faces, the ones you see standing on the corner, they never dreamed of these circumstances. Many of us had aspirations, hopes for the good life, but somewhere along the way we lost our direction, our motivation or our luck was just plain bad.

There is truly no way out now. I go to shelters and food kitchens, in addition to extending a needy hand to those who pass me on the street.

I am not one to wallow in self pity, but now it is time to stop. I can no longer have this as my way of living. I will choose the busiest corner where cars and buses and trucks will pass along quickly. I will step out in front of the next speeding truck, the impact will end my miserable life. How many of us on the corner daily feel the urge to just step out into the street.

Ah, now here comes a speeding truck, perfect, ...Adieu!

SPIRITS

No, not the imbibing kind, but the spirits that linger after death because their souls are not at peace. Their reason for "being" is still unfinished on this planet. Now the question is, do these spirits continue to mature, are they limited to their brief life experience, or do they observe and learn?

How much do they experience? Or how much are they capable of experiencing? Do they hear or merely intrinsically sense a person's inner feelings and thoughts? Do they appear at times to the 'gifted' that can actually see them in order to reveal answers to thoughts, —perhaps not answers but responses.

When the thoughts are good about someone they can appear as an apparition of light. Dark thoughts produce a somber apparition.

A memory of one gone that was loved and the light spirit appears briefly. It does not come as a Jacob Marley but in what can only be described as a spirit. It is disconcerting to think of someone or something when the dark image appears.

Usually they mean no harm, merely enlightenment on a brief thought. No, not enlightenment just an acknowledgement of the individual's thought. However, the observer can have a moment of enlightenment or clarity. They are merely responses to thought, no guidance.

All these speculations on spirits add up to nothing, but they do exist.

SISTER ADDIE

She was not in a religious order it was just that everyone called her Sister since childhood. Now it was in her thirtieth year that she quit speaking. This did not impact her work in data entry. She realized that if she thought about something before she said it, she would say nothing. So this is the path she followed. How many of us in certain situations wish that they did not have to speak?

Her only means of communication was shaking her head in the negative or nodding in the affirmative. As she thought, let the others talk, I will just listen.

The years passed and she managed very well without speaking. As she worked from home her contact with others was very limited and this suited her just fine.

On warm, sunny days she enjoyed sitting on the front porch of her house. Around the same time of day a fellow would walk by with his puppy.

Sister Addie looked forward to seeing them pass and was impressed with the gentleness and care the man took in training the puppy.

That he was being observed did not go unnoticed by William. He liked the smile that they shared when their eyes met.

One day he decided to approach Sister Addie. She tensed when she realized what was happening. Then there he was standing in front of her. What could she do? He asked softly, "you want to meet my puppy"?

In a clear, steady, enthusiastic voice she said Yes!!

SHADOWS

To look at this woman one can see a beautiful woman with striking, intelligent eyes. Questioning the look behind another's eyes is an enigma, The shadow that exists within the mind, our dark side, is our alternate side, and is not the one that we present to society. Or at least, we hope.

She has a love of art, and a failed marriage to define her. Sure, a limited view but the observation was brief. She lived in the U.S. for 7 years, married, divorced and returned to her home country. She made a life for herself there, bore a child, never remarried.

Independently, for the most part, she raised her child with plenty of love, but short of patience. The child was like that as well.

Her current relationship is "in its tenth season" she retorts to a question about her lover.

Years have passed since our initial introduction. Her beauty remains as does her joie de vivre. But to know this woman, this strong woman at the age of seventeen held her father up from the ground as he had hung himself. She cried for help, he lived.

THAT HAMILTON WOMAN

Her friends teased her and called Sarah Hamilton that when the 1941 movie was released starring Laurence Olivier and Vivian Leigh.

An overweight child she grew into a tall, thin severe looking woman that joined the navy as a nurse at the beginning of the Second World War. Whether she chose this patriotically or because she had had events in her life from which she wished to escape is not known. Probably a bit of both.

Born in 1919, she reached the tender age of twenty when she met this charming young man. He was her age, and they became engaged after a brief flurry of dates to the movies and evening walks.

Despite the brief relationship and planned marriage, she was devastated when the news of his arrest reached her.

The man to whom she believed she would spend the rest of her life was arrested for a once in a lifetime crime. He was incarcerated for riding on the public city bus and cutting the hair of women that sat in front of him.

The particulars of the case were never really released or were probably never known. But finally, he clipped his last ponytail and was discovered and this put an end to his barbering pastime.

Aunt Sarah never fully recovered from this. After the war, she married a much older man, had a son that was killed in an auto accident at the age of 16.

Not a happy life, she chain smoked until her sudden death at the dinner table. She was 92. Not long after her death, her house burned to the ground.

RUBY TUESDAY

Oh Hell, she didn't know if it was a Tuesday. But that was how she thought of it. Grace Letterle made a mistake in judgement in hiding a valuable ring in her shoe in response to a neighborhood break-in.

Grace has her peculiarities just as we all do. Those little quirks that make us individuals.

And yes, the ring was a ruby bequeathed to her by her Grandmother. She wore the ring, with its guard, on the middle finger of her left hand.

In a spurt of purging, Grace spent an evening preparing a large donation for a local charity organization. Forgetting about the ring in the shoe, she placed the loafers in the donation bag. Within the one shoe was a sock with the ruby as well as a gold coral ring.

Grace cried when she realized what she had done. As she walked to the closet door to find the shoe and put the ring on, the reality of the situation came crashing down on her.

Feeling bourgeois and repentant, she took advice and claimed the "donation" on her taxes.

Ironically, seven years later her cousin passed and left her a ruby ring. Grace looks at this as providence or maybe just coming full circle in a world fraught with complexities.

These days the only thing Grace puts in her shoes are her feet.

ROY LEE

Roy Lee was an innocent. He knew very little about the ways of people. As a meter reader for the local gas and electric company he worked alone and had little contact with his fellow meter readers.

He could be seen every month silently, slowly walking into people's backyards to check their meters. The job suited him; he had only worked there a short time.

Unbeknownst to Roy Lee, a woman had watched for him routinely, although his arrival times varied. This woman, a self-proclaimed femme fatale had designs on Roy Lee. This attraction did not grow out of loneliness. She simply thought he would be someone she could toy with for awhile.

As he entered the backyard she saw him pass by her kitchen window. She just happened to wander into the yard to check her bird feeder. She boldly placed herself in front of Roy Lee before he rapidly exited the yard trying to avoid contact with this woman. This did not deter her as she blocked his way. Standing face to face she placed her hand over his pounding heart and asked him his name.

These "chance" meetings continued and Roy Lee never questioned the odd coincidences that she would appear at the back door to send a greeting. Then one warm spring day she invited him to her house for that very evening. She could practically hear the trap shut as he nervously accepted the invitation.

Roy Lee left with only one thought in mind— how would he get through the night. He didn't want to hurt her feelings, but he was quite upset at the prospects of spending an evening with her.

Arriving promptly at the appointed hour, he watched the sun pass gently from the sky. He entered the house. She welcomed him with a shark smile and gestured toward the pillows on the floor of the living room. He noticed there was no couch. So he seated himself, thinking 'Oh what the heck I will not refuse a glass of wine.'

Roy Lee could not help noticing the way she was dressed. He knew nothing of fashion but thought she looked lovely in the flowing lavender rayon gown which clung to her form as she bent forward to hand him a glass of wine. Romance was far from his mind as he took in all the lit candles around the room.

By the time Roy Lee had his third glass of wine, he was not uncomfortable with her sliding next to him on the large pillow. She began nuzzling his neck. As she moved ever closer and he tried to move away, a candle fell from the shelf above her head. It tumbled from its place to land on the rayon ribbon in her hair and rolled down to the rayon dress. She jumped up as the flames engulfed her. There was nothing Roy Lee could do but gape and gasp.

The news story of this broke and his fellow workers took note and treated Roy Lee kindly. He never got over the night. Sometimes he did wonder the irony of dying in the living room.

THE ROCK STAR

He wasn't just a rock star, it was Ray Davies of the Kinks. And her plan to contact him worked beautifully.

Each year she receives a calendar of postcards depicting villages in England from a friend living there. The village, Lilly says with great pride, is considered the prettiest in England. Located in North Yorkshire, the little town of Thornton-le-Dale is truly a lovely spot on the planet.

So, to the subject at hand, she contacted Lilly asking her to mail her a British postage stamp. Her friend did and the plan was set in motion.

She had been writing to the Rock Star for about a year at this time. She had begun this one-sided correspondence after finding she related to much of his music. By merely calling the publisher of his autobiography in New York, she was assured they would forward all his mail to him in North London. She had sent him cards from Paris and other destinations to which she traveled.

Tired of the writing and not knowing whether he received her letters, she decided to mail him one of the postcards depicting an English village with the following message. On the card was her address.

She offered him several options on the postcard. She asked for a response to "Yes, I receive your letters feel free to write again", or "Yes, I receive your letters and frankly my dear, I don't give a damn," and finally "I receive your letters, now go away."

Months passed with no word. Then to her delight there was the long-anticipated postcard with a check mark beside "Feel free to write again." So, she did...

THE POSTMAN NEVER RINGS ANYMORE

Emma Stokes had been an employee of the Post Office 7 years. For the past 5 years she remained delivering mail in the same neighborhood. To some this may seem monotonous but for Emma it was the beginning of an obsessive preoccupation.

She scarcely knew the names but knew that 2903 Brewster received mail from other parts of the world. Naturally her imagination took flight with these sometimes ornate stamps from other lands unknown to her.

With her Eleanor Rigby kind of existence, Emma found refuge in her own mind. Rarely bored, she invented scenarios at the slightest occurrence in her daily life.

The brick house at 2909 was so inviting that Emma actually took notice of the myriad of seed catalogues that arrived. She imagined the backyard as a lovely version of a Maxfield Parrish painting. It was always to her delight when she spied the bulb boxes that arrived with regularity.

The disturbing house at 400 Bailey kept having letters returned because of the lack of postage. In this case Emma naturally imagined the worst. The home was overgrown and neglected.

Then one day a letter was returned from Belgium—the letter refused, return to sender appeared on the outside of the envelope.

Not only was imagination a part of Emma's character but empathy was as well. She became distraught at the thought of someone in pain or having difficulty.

As the seasons pass Emma's footsteps grow slower and her imagination lags. The neighborhood changed as the years passed. The foreign letters ceased after the inhabitant of 2903 Brewster moved with a forwarding address in Botswana. The home of the avid garden stayed consistently beautiful if not more so as the plants matured and filled the landscape. The house of mystery and abandonment burned to the ground from an electrical fire.

One bleak winter morning, Emma never awoke from her peaceful slumber; her life ended due to an aneurism. Quick and painless.

The objects of Emma's fascination over the years only noticed that their mail delivery time had changed.

A MEMBER OF THE DEADLY NIGHTSHADE FAMILY

Her nom de plume was Fancy. Her questionable manner of going through life delighted many onlookers.

I can't give my impression upon first meeting her. After time I noticed she seemed to always be a tad nonplussed in conversation. Her smile belied her intentions, I have no doubt.

But as to the nature of her intentions, I dare not venture a guess. One evening while preparing dinner, she inadvertently sliced a daffodil bulb into her stir-fry thinking it was a shallot. It poisoned her and she died.

After her untimely death, all was open to speculation: Did she really? She said that? Now how could she have known?

As was her choice, she was cremated and let go out of the window of a car going 80 mph along a forgotten road in the southeast of the county. She had no last wishes, only to be forgotten.

THE NEO-MEN AT THE DOOR

It was a bright spring day, late morning when the bell rang.

There were two of them standing there. And naturally, I wondered what do they want, as I peered at them through the glass storm door.

He began his spiel immediately—slightly nervous more false bravado than anything else. The other stood to the side merely listening, contributing nothing to the dialogue that proceeded. They sell magazines and said much of the proceeds went to a "nebulous" good cause.

In the mood for banter, I questioned him occasionally as he spoke on various topics.

He was asking for $25 which would ensure I would receive numerous well-known magazines from Elle to Vanity Fair.

As we spoke the topic of my occupation arose. When I revealed that I worked in recordings for the blind, his expression changed. He told me he had a close friend that was blind. The friend receives the recordings. They sauntered away.

I think at that time he felt the pangs of conscience. I come to this conclusion because he had been to my sister's house several days before. She gave him a check for the requested amount.

She told me later that feeling suspicious, she canceled the check. She was told by the bank officer that many checks made payable to this fellow had passed through the bank and added that many people had stopped payment on their checks.

Having heard this, I remembered that he decided that I didn't need magazines after all.

IN THE MIRROR

Lilly Fleury was in her later years. She had a pleasant face, a pretty face actually. In her home was a large bathroom mirror which was lit by round globe lights across the top. This was the only mirror she looked in from the morning ablutions to evening preparations for bed. She would scrutinize her appearance in the mirror before leaving for the day. The gentle light softened and concealed the ravages of time and in her mind, she still looked quite lovely. That demeanor of beauty, she carried with her when she went out into the world.

Cursed by one of the Seven Deadly Sins, her sin was that of pride. Pride in her appearance, her beauty, her countenance, which was confirmed as she gazed at herself in the mirror.

Her daily activities were simple tasks involving shopping for the weekly groceries and maybe visiting a plant shop. For one of these outings, she added to her list of "things to do" including a visit to a local home improvement retailer to purchase a hammer as the handle on her old one had broken. Walking towards the hardware section of the store, she had to pass the bathroom fixtures including the vanities. She turned her head glimpsing the face of an old, wrinkled woman which startled her when she realized it was her own face under the bright incandescent light.

She was reminded of the old film star Rita Hayworth that covered all the mirrors in her house in order to avoid seeing herself and what the passage of time had done to her lovely features.

With resolve, yet fascination, she peered more closely into the face, the puffy eyes, the pale drawn features and slowly, sadly, she turned away. Next, she approached the checkout lane and purchased the hammer. She thanked the clerk in a barely audible voice.

She entered the house and had her Amazon Echo repeat playing July Collins' "Who Knows Where the Time Goes". Walking into the bathroom, she took the newly purchased hammer and smashed the mirror, watching it as it shattered and fell to the floor. Lifting a shard of glass, she quickly cut deeply into her wrists. The blood flowed quickly from her as she lay dying upon the remains of the broken mirror. Her life faded away, like a flower that shrivels and dies on the stem.

AFTER MIDNIGHT

Found in a shelter, this six-year-old black male cat won the staff's heart with his affectionate nature. He was renamed JackJack by this staff a moniker from The Incredibles movies. Once in his new home he was renamed Midnight a name to which he responded immediately. This was perhaps his former name in his home in rural Eastern Kentucky. The staff also called him an Appalachian Mountain cat.

Midnight's original home was with a young boy who was plagued by numerous allergies, one of which turned out to be his cat. Next Midnight found a home with Juliet Edmonson, an older woman, living in a small cottage. Midnight was her sole companion. He observed her as she practiced her daily morning yoga. Midnight particularly liked savasana or resting pose at the end of the practice. As Juliet lay with arms extended, palms open, Midnight would nestle his head in her hand. She always responded with a gentle squeeze. Then one morning there was no responding squeeze, and Midnight was placed in a local shelter. Days passed and no one expressed interest in him so it was decided that he should be transferred to a larger city with a greater population.

Two weeks passed and no one wanted him despite his winning ways. Then one day he found his home. His new owner found him gentle and enjoyed how he would chirrup little sounds in her direction. Often pet and owner would stare at one another for long moments. They were sizing each other up.

Indulging in anthropomorphic thought, it appears to the human observer that Midnight knows he has a new home and is quite pleased. Unlike many humans and animals this little fellow has never known mistreatment. It is refreshing to witness such trust from one so small and relatively defenseless.

Now liberties were taken creating Midnight's previous life but why not? It was something to do on a rainy day!!

A BEAUTIFUL PHOTOGRAPH

It was a beautiful photograph, a hauntingly beautiful photograph. It was taken in 1894 and I know I took that photograph, although it was 126 years ago. I cannot deny it is mad to think this, yet I believe we all have our times of madness.

What is her story, what is her name, this child in the old photograph. Does her story differ from countless others? We live, we die. During that time we compile a surfeit of memories. As we grow older, we find we visit these memories more often, perhaps more readily, in an attempt to escape our present reality.

Her name was Mary Russell. Raised in Lexington with her aunt and uncle the DeHavens, she was the only child from parents James Russell and Betty Morgan Russell. The DeHavens became her parents after the untimely death of James and Betty.

Following her marriage to Marion Bicknell, Mary lived in Lagrange , Kentucky a town in Oldham County. Nothing is known of her childhood. She was born November 3, 1887 and died December 17, 1920

September of 1912 , Mary gave birth to
Marion Junior. A healthy boy who grew beneath the
watchful, protective eye of his Mother. Eight years
later, Mary gave birth to a daughter, Elisabeth. The
son adored the Mother and his newborn sister and
life continued in familial happiness.

Then, there was Mary's illness. She was 33
with her daughter not yet one year old. Mary was
hospitalized in Louisville under a doctor's care.
Following instructions from the doctor, Mary was
administered a morphine injection. It killed her. She
died before her husband reached home.

So yes, I took her photograph
metaphorically. I took her story, her short life and
shared it.

May her image never grace a Cracker Barrel
wall.

WHERE DOES LOVE COME FROM?

Their names: Rebel Monk and Rosa Bonheur. They knew nothing of one another's existence. Rebel flew commercial helicopters, selling rides to anxious customers. The copter was housed at a small local airport. Rosa lived nearby said airport.

An avid gardener, she spent hours tending the plants. As one day would have it, while hovering over her neighborhood, before landing, Rebel spotted the graceful figure in her yard. That was it. He had to meet her. Having the name Rebel did not develop timidity in this young man. So, he set out to meet her in her natural habitat. Rebel left the airport after landing and hoping that she was still outside, saw her and approached.

Rosa was wary of the man walking up to her but stood her ground. Their eyes met, sparks. In gentlemanly fashion he introduced himself and a conversation ensued.

As is the way of things, they sought out commonalities. Likes and dislikes were rapidly discussed. When the topic turned to movies, the same likes were remarkable.

They both liked Quentin Tarantino and could quip to one another lines from *Pulp Fiction*.

When they both came to agree on *Natural Born Killers*, it was love.

No, they became nothing so predictable as serial killers, quite the opposite. As their love grew, so did their taste in movies. Rosa, with her French background, was drawn to war movies about the two world wars. The fateful night they watched the 1982 movie, *Sophie's Choice* about a holocaust survivor, sealed their combined fates.

Their next movie choice was the 1991 film, *The Fisher King* with Robin Williams. A lasting impression was made when Williams, as the homeless Perry, is stabbed by ruffians: he thanks them. It was no coincidence to seek out a Robin William's movie in light of his suicide. They became obsessed with dying.

The decision was made. They knew deep in their souls that they were nihilists. Life had little purpose so why continue the daily discomfort of merely trying to exist.

They chose the method used by Sophie and Nathan, and ingested sodium cyanide. They lay in one another's arms, looking into one another's eyes as the light slowly faded from them. They left no note, no parting words. Sadly, they thought their leaving made the world a better place.

LOUIE

You could say her flaming red hair defined her and it was a pleasant surprise to find that her husband's name was Red.

They could have been anyone's neighbors; they were friendly and quiet and would warn children to stay away from Brandy, their huge St. Bernard residing in the backyard. Thus, the yard became a mysterious place not often visited. Then one day a small concrete pool was added, upon which floated multicolored glass globes. The fear of Brandy was overcome in order to gaze upon the aquatic scene.

Then there was the day Louie stepped on the rake which flew up and hit her directly in the face, breaking her glasses. This was a memorable incident to witness for a young one.

On warm summer evenings, with windows open the nearby neighbors could hear Red playing the organ. The melodious tunes brought serenity to an already tranquil evening.

Then one morning Red did not awaken. His death was peaceful, like his music.

Louie never removed his slippers that remained by the bed. She spent solitary nights alone in her chair with her memories.

Within a few years, Louie died; the once brilliant red hair now white with care and sorrow.

Today as I look at the necklace she gave me, I wonder, does anyone else ever think of Louie and Red?

LITERATURE

Why do you read? It is in order to look at the world through the eyes, through the words, of someone else. It can change perspectives, can leave lasting impressions. Traveling through time, through emotions, one can leave their surroundings and experience feelings that would not ordinarily be experienced in their seemingly solitary lives.

With a good reading lamp beside you, you can become an armchair traveler. A voyeur into the lives of others, their emotions, their thoughts and their motivations. The last, the most telling.

Open a book, and you open a world. With each page you step more deeply into the tale being told. With a well-told story, you laugh at moments of levity and feel downcast as circumstances become bleak in the tale.

We can end a book feeling enlightened and with a sense of fulfillment on the completion of a well written oeuvre.

So, what is the motivation in writing this? It is the result of a conversation I had a year ago with a tax accountant that was complaining that his son was studying literature at the university. This is my response though a bit late.

THE LIMB WALKER

His name was Branch Dubois and he depended on the kindness of strangers. Strangers were his bread and butter. His parents gave him the name as a symbol of a continuation of the family tree. They had no idea that the name would also lead to his occupation. As an arborist, Branch found himself at elevated heights in the trees above the suburban neighborhoods of the northeastern town.

At an early age Branch showed his preference for the outdoors. Late in the night his father would find Branch's bed empty. The boy had taken to the woods and hid from his father behind the nearby trees which cast long shadows into the night.

Falling and weather were the two major hazards in Branch's line of work. An independent contractor, he worked his own hours and did well as word of mouth spread of his abilities as an arborist. He enjoyed the challenge of the large, tall trees. His duties included trimming and tree removal and his opinion was respected and business grew.

Were his customers strangers? No more than anyone else is a stranger to another. Branch never questioned the depths of a relationship with the people for whom he was employed.

71

Always a dreamer, one would not characterize Branch as totally aware of his surroundings. Sure-footed and lucky he found his way around a tree much to his satisfaction. However, he did take chances, tempting the fates.

The day was dark and threatening and he took no notice as he ascended the tall mountain ash. His thoughts were on his work as he carefully made his way upwards. The lightning strike took him quickly, he neither knew nor felt anything, it was so quick.

His was a short life, he made no real, lasting impact on the community save for the trees he trimmed.   He had no children and thus ended the family tree. Eric Neuebaum bought his equipment and began an arborist business for himself much as Branch had done. Never as reliable as Branch, the business failed and Eric became a house painter.

LIAR'S LOVE

They knew one another at University,
Edward was drawn to Raymond immediately. It was
a secret love. Now, how they became involved is
unknown to anyone. For a brief time they were
lovers, perhaps, only once to satisfy their needs.

Raymond could not live the life Edward
envisioned. Raymond wanted a wife, children and
what would he tell his parents?

So, Edward killed himself and Raymond
married and had children. He dedicated his book to
Edward.

JUKE BOX HERO

He liked to think of himself as a shopkeeper. His music store thrived as he specialized in seldom found music. He watched old I Love Lucy shows and the original Star Trek.

Artie Russell had a peculiar manner in regard to women. He kept the shop's AC turned down because he wanted to see how the female customers' breasts reacted to the cold temperatures.

It was a juvenile practice and no one knew he did this as he had no friends in which to confide. So when Carlene Drapper entered his store, he was not prepared for her. A Goodwill shopper, she actually wore a Raspberry Beret. He marveled at her stride then was taken aback when she strolled over to the thermostat and turned up the AC unit.

It was love at first sight for him and he remembered "the customer is always right."

ILLUSIONS OF AN INTROVERT

Researching the word illusion reveals it is defined as a distortion of the senses which can reveal how the human brain normally organizes and interprets sensory stimulation. Although illusions distort our perception of reality, they are generally shared by most people.

That is the definition she found and felt mollified that it is common and not something particular to people of her nature. Yet, then again, how many are of her nature? She knew her sensory stimulation was truly engaged when hearing music. She retreated into music; it was her time machine.

She begged off from social gatherings and found she was most comfortable just one on one. She avoided too much stimulation from taste, or smell or touch.

As each day passed, she retreated more into her music. Her tastes varied and she enjoyed thinking of songs remembered from years past. She began her day with music, and listened all day long. It was her repellent against life.

Her hearing loss came on gradually. Initially it was of no matter to her, it made it easier to end phone conversations. Sudden sensorineural hearing loss which is commonly known as sudden deafness struck her. She was suddenly in a world without sound. Sadly, it drove her mad. She neglected herself to the point of starvation. She died in her bed, alone and without an accompanying song for her departure.

IBBY AND BILL

High school sweethearts, their romance started at the age of 16. Ibby wore a gold locket with Bill's picture inside. They never dreamed a world war would separate them.

It was 1940 and at the age of 20 they married. Like other couples, they shared their lives and enjoyed one another's company. Weekends would often find them at the local movie house.

By December of 1941, the country was drawn into a world war.

Bill joined the army and was sent abroad. They promised to write and did so loyally. At this time letters were closely watched, and passages often redacted. It was forbidden to reveal locations, so that topic was avoided.

Ibby could not conceal her worry for Bill's well-being. Sensing this, Bill decided to let her know his whereabouts. Feigning sentimentalism, Bill wrote remember the last movie we saw? Ibby remember, it was the 1938 movie Algiers with Hedy Lamar and Charles Boyer. With that she knew where Bill was; he was in Northern Africa.

Bill survived the war and returned home to Ibby. Their 28-year marriage ended tragically with Bill's death at 47. Ibby was never the same. She lived 45 more years feeling this loss daily.

HIM/HER

He lived his life the best he could. As he often said, "I bought a house and paid it off and I bought a car and paid it off." Is that how someone would describe their life? A life filled with responsibilities.

A child entered his life as a newborn, his son. He played the father role and set aside his music. He was a gifted guitar player. Just took to it. He never tried to read music, was one that could play by ear, a natural talent.

The first marriage lasted 17 years and in order to have a successful marriage, he put his guitar in the closet and did not return to it until, as he said, "it was not another woman, it was another man. " He stayed out all night playing his guitar with one of his friends. It was the end of his marriage.

After 12 years, he married again. His wife loved that he played guitar. They spent evenings in local bars as he played music with friends.

Then she came along. A memory now a reality from his past. He claimed that she had broken his heart. And in a sense, she did. She knew he was married and did not want to cause trouble.

They met several times and talked but it just could not be.

Never wanting to hurt him again, she had a symbol of his spirit animal added to a gravestone she had had put in a family plot years ago. He never knew, and their lives went on.

THE GROCERY CLERK

He is always at the checkout lane and ready with a smile and conversation. He asks about the family and comments on some of the various purchases.

As it was nearing the Thanksgiving holiday a mutual wish was extended for a festive time. He comments that he would work as he always works on holidays. His mother and grandmother gone, he prefers the company of passing strangers or the exchange of a friendly smile with a recognized face.

He always remarks on the peanut butter cookie mix purchase and often will exclaim "I am going to get some of those cookie mixes too." He reveals that he often finds people's purchases interesting and revealing.

He relates the story of a purchase of motor oil and beer, or when someone bought only lemons and salt. This interest is only passing but can occupy his thoughts as he mechanically passes the groceries over the scanner.

The friendly nature and easy candor draw interest on the part of the keen observer. Naturally questions form making the observer imagine the life and motivations of this grocery clerk named, Mark.

On Mark's somber days, he says that his heart breaks for the child within us all. Why does he say this in such a melancholy manner? What has touched his life in such a way to form those desolate thoughts?

There are others in line and his comment really sought no response. The next customer merely shrugs, anxious to get home to the 6:00 news.

Day after day Mark was longing for an adventurous life, one of stealing from the rich and giving to the poor. That was the day he began sliding groceries past the scanner avoiding the ring up charge. He only chose those that looked in need of a hand up.

This life of Robin Hood continued for several months. Then one day Mark decided to move on. He gave no notice just failed to return. As it was summer, he began working for a lawn service and forgot about his quest to feed the poor.

The grocery did see an improvement in profit after his disappearance, but surprisingly they never associated it with Mark.

Now he spends his days nurturing and cultivating landscapes.

THE GODLESS ONE

"I came along somewhere between the resurrection and the insurrection," she would tell people but was never quite sure what she meant. She just liked the way the two words rhymed.

From time to time she would quip, "I have no empathy because I have no sympathy."
She took pride in her attitude and relished the idea that she could upset or unnerve people. She claimed her goal in life was to amuse and to confuse.

Her general indifference was not an inherent trait, though innate, voicing her thoughts came slowly. Hesitant to challenge other's faith, she now became militant. She struggled with her feeling, yet always came up with the same results, "there is no god."

She admired Immanuel Kant who conceived of God as a "postulate of practical reason," that it is an idea created by human beings to lend legitimacy to their autonomous, rational, ethical system.

She read various religious discussions which included Jonathan Edwards' *Sinners in the Hands of an Angry God.* She scoffed at his presumptions. In further pursuit of knowledge, she studied

Contemporary Jewish thought at the university. She found it refreshing to study a Jewish rabbi, that denied the existence of God until he was on his deathbed and recanted his statement, "Just in case." Her only reaction was a loud, resounding oath, "chickenshit."

FREEDOM FROM FEAR

When even crossing the street became a problem, I began to take my irrational fears seriously. I anticipate danger and obsess on the consequences.

After much deliberation, it became apparent professional help was needed. Seeking a therapist seemed like the next obvious step.

In an attempt to come to terms in watching the film *Fearless* , I was persuaded to move forward with my plan. So, my first course of action was to find the therapist.

Following the usual channels, asking friends, insurance listings and so on led me to Emma Deacon, a nurse practitioner. As was discussed by us, there are many medical approaches to conquering fear. Such meds as Trazodone, an anxiety medication, and others such as Meloxicam and Amitriptyline were also suggested by Emma. Along with the medicinal treatment, books were recommended to overcome panic and anxiety.

The reality of my fears told me that my case was not going to be resolved with drugs or books; I needed a serious reversal of emotion. Researching my malady, because it is truly an illness, I found that fear is closely related to, but should be distinguished from, the emotion, anxiety. Anxiety occurs as the result of threats that are perceived to be uncontrollable or unavoidable.

Looking further revealed the thought that love is the most powerful emotion and that fear, after all, is a negative emotion. Not surprising really as fear is a primal instinct. It is an innate fear. Humans are born with only two innate fears: the fear of falling and the fear of loud sounds. The fear of falling is an instinct necessary for the survival of many species. When a loud sound is heard, it most likely is met with a flight or fight response.

Finding that in areas of my life fear can paralyze my actions, I resolved to seek help for my pernicious condition. Firmly believing that counseling had not relieved my sense of impending doom around every corner, I made a list of my most prevalent fears and decided to attempt to conquer these foreboding feelings.

The first major problem arises in trying to carry on a long conversation with someone. I fear that I would insult, misspeak or even put myself in danger. These fears would creep into my thoughts, my psyche. My next greatest fear was that people could read my thoughts. This fear at times was so overpowering that I had to talk myself off the ledge. Accompanying this was the certainty that certain sounds would occur as a response to my thoughts. Fear of traveling and meeting people, people I already knew could terrorize me. Along with this, was the feeling that other people would respond to me not in their words but the words of those of an unseen force. It may all be just a matter of self-obsession, but it was more than I could deal with on a daily basis.

As I found, normally, there are two amygdalae per person with one amygdala on each side of the brain. They are thought to be a part of the limbic system within the brain which is responsible for emotion, survival instincts, and memory. My research also revealed people who have an overactive amygdala may have a heightened fear response causing increased anxiety in social situations. Fear hormones are secreted by the adrenal gland, an endocrine gland located on top of the kidneys. The fear hormones circulate through the blood stream to all cells of the body. One fascinating case involved the removal of the amygdala in an effort to treat severe epilepsy. The patient became a hyper empath. Little else was told about this strange case.

So, the die is cast, the decision made. I will seek help in the form of a doctor to perform this life changing operation. I need to persuade a neurologist that this operation could be beneficial not only to me but a population of those experiencing such overwhelming fear.

I decided the best approach in engaging a prospective doctor was to be straight forward and hopefully to persuade this person to want to help me and to help others.

By a simple twist of fate, I have found that the patient that received surgery due to severe epilepsy was a neurologist. Naturally, I feel this person would sympathize with me and perform the necessary surgery.

After an appointment was arranged, I tried to wait patiently to present my illness and seek help.

All hope depends on whether this doctor will truly recognize my dilemma and be willing to remove one half of the amygdalae freeing me from constant fear.

Finally, the day has arrived for the appointment. When the doctor enters the room, the fear I feel is the fear the doctor feels and the moment is momentous.

It does not take long for the doctor to realize what I am seeking. An agreement is made, and a neurological surgery is scheduled.

Checking into the hospital went smoothly and as I recline in the bed my heart is beating erratically and the terror becomes real. I jump from the bed, screaming to be released. I run down the stairwell, the doors opening at my approach. I exit the hospital and gallop into the street. I run towards the traffic, cars swerving to avoid contact. Then one final scream as the oncoming car mows me down.

As this is such a rapid departure from a happy solution. There exists the possibility, in this best of all possible worlds, that I decide against the surgery and begin to work on my own recovery from a life of fear. Small steps take me to the realization that alone I can overcome fear by facing each one individually. I begin self-analysis and see a brighter future.

FERAL

Homeless is his name and he has been treated badly by a previous owner. Now, I don't own Homeless, I feed Homeless, and often he allows me to watch him display his catch. He hunts nights.

It occurs to me that he is similar in nature to someone that I know, someone I care for, and I find myself projecting this animal's characteristics to those of this human.

Yes, a foolish notion but I find it is easier to relate to the animal than the human. So can one attribute animal characteristics to a human, a sort of reverse anthropomorphizing? A broader definition or personification is not appropriate as this coincidence defies definition.

A feral cat is an un-owned domestic cat that lives outdoors and avoids human contact. It does not allow itself to be touched or handled. This sounds like a description of my human rather than Homeless.

By definition, a feral person is one that has lived isolated from human contact. This appears to happen in the case of children or the" Wild Child": cases. My human chose this isolation and as an adult prefers to have no more contact with others than necessary.

A most telling reaction is how the human, and the cat can react to my thoughts; thereby, getting a certain vibe from the emotional atmosphere.

People can be described as being nervous as a cat. So again, not too unusual to attribute or find animal-like traits in my human. Yes, it seems to be an internal argument over this attribution of cat-like characteristics to a human, but after all we too are basically animals with our fight or flight instinct.

Thinking of examples for this observation several instances come to mind. As I sit idly with Homeless next to me, thoughts drifting from subject to subject, a negative thought suddenly passes through my mind. Homeless reacts. He will always move away from me quickly as my reverie has disturbed his sleep. On the rare occasion, I am with my human, he is jumpy and if he senses a negative feeling from me he becomes agitated just like Homeless.

Difficult to admit, but I find myself calling both of them, buddy. They both seem to like it, so I will continue this harmless practice.

It just seems to be a remarkable coincidence that the days Homeless acts snippy, my human is in the same mood. This has occurred enough times not to be random.

Often, I feel both Human and Homeless wish that I practice therianthropy or shape shifting to become an animal. Homeless gives me a look as if to say, "I wish you were a girl kitty." And in general, my human prefers four legged creatures to the two legged variety

So tonight, as Homeless saunters into the house he is particularly affectionate. Now I wonder what this could mean. As I go for Homeless' treat there is a gentle tap at the door. As I approach the

door I open to my Human, my response? Come on
in human, are you hungry?

FEAR

After her 13th birthday, which was very bad due to a chimpanzee, a clown, and an assortment of rubber snakes, Trisha became triskaidekaphobic. Her fear of the number 13 formed her life after that day. This fear can be passed down in families, but this was not the case with Trisha.

Convinced this fear could be conquered, her parents looked into the ancient history connected to the fear. The oldest known reference comes from the Mesopotamian code of Hammurabi, a Babylonian code of law that dates to approximately 1760 BC. The laws are numbered but the number 13 is omitted. This can be found today in the omission of the 13th floor in buildings. None of the practical facts associated with triskaidekaphobia made any impression on Trisha.

Time passed and she found life not so difficult as decisions were made avoiding possible confrontations with the number 13.

So, in the year 2020 on November 13th, a Friday, she was able not only to leave the house but to proceed to a building with the street number of 1313.

Trisha felt nothing as the car struck her as she exited her vehicle. One of the witnesses told police over the woman's dead body, I got the license number 513-13. The number was duly noted, and the crowd dispersed.

FATED

He will kill me; I know he will. I want him to kill me, and I would thank him as I draw my last breath. Death has never been a matter of caprice, a whim, no, it is a state of unconsciousness that I dream about. A profound sleep from which I can never return.

Once before, I asked someone to kill me. It was years ago and after his shock subsided, he never was quite comfortable with me again.

This time it will be because I have manipulated him; enraged him, to kill me.

He is a jealous sort, and I will taunt him with trysts, and flagrant unfaithfulness. I will flirt and lead him on and then disappear with someone else.

Sending him the two Browning poems, "My Last Duchess" and Porphyria's Lover, should have planted the idea in his mind. He will take my life with his own hands. He will be relieved to snuff out my life. He will no longer be tormented by my infidelities.

Ah, there he is now, I hear the familiar creak on the stairs as he approaches. The rapid knock on the door will not be immediately answered. Let him boil, let that temper take over.

The persistent knocks must be answered, or neighbors will become alarmed. My fate awaits me. With relief I will walk towards the door, open it and bare my slender neck to receive his angry hands. Goodbye, I can truly say with joy.

EDITH MALLONI

She thought deceased people after the funeral were merely parked, they rise just as Christ did. Yet, her mind would reel at her daily premonitions.

Talking to her was always a chore, as she would tell what she considered to be funny anecdotes.

She always wore the same pair of earrings and smelled of the face lotion she applied every morning.

Everything she attempted to do she always claimed was a labor of love. Her efforts on tasks never failed to amuse passersby as she wrangled a particular weed growing in the front yard.

There was a time she enjoyed the company of others, women and men. She could be a clever conversationalist.

When she died at 93 there were few people to tell as by this time, she knew no one. Her solitary life was focused largely on her trying to cope with everyday tasks.

As her life flashed before her it was made up of brief vignettes and gladly was accompanied with laughter.

DRAWN

In the words of Prince "she came in through the outdoor", no raspberry beret but a presence he was drawn to.

A forced conversation ensued, and he got few responses to his questions. His request to see her was only met with reluctance. In her world, matters don't proceed in such a manner.

Their paths crossed again, and she was not so distant at this chance meeting. Surprised, not really pleased, she conceded to speak with him. It was an unsatisfactory conversation and they parted.

Years passed and he never saw her again. Then one evening he was invited to a small get together. It was her face that greeted him as he entered the door.

What he wanted to know about her became clear when he glanced at the table that held her glass of wine. She was using the book of Portuguese Love Sonnets as a coaster. He knew all chance was lost.

CONTENTS OF THE ABANDONED DRAWER

The drawer was discovered in a house in which the occupants had recently moved. It held little interest except to those with an inquisitive mind and a fertile imagination. There was the incense, Gorilla glue, several programs from memorial services and miscellaneous items that make up an abandoned drawer.

Glance at them and travel to their origins— back from where they came. Each item original, just as each fingerprint or snowflake. The moment of acquisition, take time to reflect on the contents, for they speak volumes to the observer. Hurt and joy perhaps, but communication none the less.

Don't pass it by, look at the abandoned drawer and reflect.

DOLDRUMS

As an adult, she never changed her habits; her way to go through each day. Mornings were always the same, she even awoke at the same time on the weekends.

Bed making was the first way to address the day and the daily ablutions consisted of brushing the teeth for two minutes, she counted them, and then rinsing her face three times with cold water, then lathering with apricot soap. The final rinse, lotion and a touch of mascara completed the ritual.

She worked for a Certified Public Accountant. As his assistant, she had various responsibilities. Always cheerful when she answered the phone, the last few months a certain tone of boredom had crept into her voice.

She often sought refuge in music. Country music helped relieve the tedious days. At last she decided this is an opportunity to break free from the doldrums that make up her life. She told herself, it is 2017, I have worked this job for 5 years and I need to look forward to each day, not dread them. I need the prospect of something fun to do.

She began researching nearby concerts. Her search resulted in finding a concert in Paradise,

Nevada. How perfect!! One of the scheduled artists was Jason Aldean who was going to close the show.

She couldn't contain her excitement, as she made the necessary travel arrangements and bought her ticket for the Oct. 1st show. Humming gently to herself, thinking, this is a show to die for. And she did.

THE SAFETY DEPOSIT BOX

The sisters received word of their mother's passing. They made the necessary travel plans and left for her Florida home within days.

Matters were much as they expected with nosy neighbors and the curious handyman awaiting their arrival.

The amount of time spent there would be short, just sorting papers and preparing the house to be sold. However, it was the trip to the bank that left them somewhat surprised, or better yet, puzzled.

When the deposit box was pulled from the wall of boxes, one sister commented to the other about the surprising weight of the safety deposit box. When the box was opened, they looked at one another bewildered. Inside were 2 heavy doorknobs, one brass the other crystal and a seal with their mother's name. Now they knew the cause of the weight but as the older sister questioned ...why?

The younger sister supplied the possible reason. She wanted the bank employees to think she had gold or something of some weighty value inside the box. Tragically, all her self-worth was tied up in another fabrication which they knew made up her life.

A DARK DELUSION

Photography was his pastime, no, more than a pastime, a passion. His subjects varied but there was one destination that was his favorite spot. It was the cemetery. And in that cemetery, there was one particular monument where he spent a great deal of time. Yes, it was an obsession. He loved the tragic face of the mourning woman, her head bowed, leaning against a cross. The icon of suffering.

His visits increased to daily visits. He photographed her from all angles—repeated shots to deepen the study. Thoughts of her were often present away from the cemetery. His girlfriend became jealous of the way in which he described her sorrowful stance. It was apparent he was enamored by this woman of stone.

One morning he awoke excitedly as he had plans for an entire series of black and white photographs of her. He set out early in order to capture the light. Enroute to the cemetery on this bright spring day, the automobile accident in which he was involved caused a blunt trauma to his head. It was immediate blindness. He would never gaze upon her lovely form again.

BY ANY OTHER NAME

Delores Whitemoon is not her given name or not the one given at birth. Delores gave herself that name after seeing it online. It is the name of a little-known author. It does not matter about Delores' real name as she only uses it on legal documents. So, as she wants, Delores Whitemoon is what she is called.

Delores has a fear of sharks to the point she cannot look at photos of them in magazines. During her brief marriage her husband derived pleasure from forcing her to look at shark pictures. This was not a move to eliminate her fear but enjoyment in watching her cringe.

This unhappy relationship ended in divorce, and couple parted ways. The only final word she received about her ex was in a Christmas card from an acquaintance. Enclosed was a newspaper article detailing the events in her ex-spouse's life. The ex-husband remarried, and the couple adopted a girl with whom he apparently had a physical relationship. As unfortunately happens in the U.S. these problems are often solved with gunfire. The man shot the girl and then himself in the front yard of their home. Merry Christmas!

THE DOWNSTAIRS NEIGHBOR

She never noticed when he moved in below her in the fourplex apartment building. Many had lived there beneath her as she had occupied the apartment for many years. The small three-room apartment had a fireplace and the dwelling was all she needed or wanted.

Once a census taker questioned her about the neighbor, but all she could say was that his name was Dean and that they rarely crossed paths.

A few years passed uneventfully, then suddenly she began receiving dating suggestions in the mail. This is before dating became such a business and an online affair. Then phone calls began. At the beginning she paid little attention to the mail and phone calls but as it continued, she became non-plussed by the persistence.

She decided to confide in the woman that lived across the hall and was told that it was Dean that had submitted her name to the dating service. The woman explained that he had taken her mail from the hallway mailbox to get her full name and thus the deed was done. Silently she questioned why the woman had never told of this, no wish to get involved or waiting to see if there would be an outcome from this meddling probably.

She wasn't angry just never understood why someone would intrude on her solitary life in such a manner. Eventually, receiving no response, the mail and calls quit.

A few more years passed, and she moved away. She never spoke to him about this and only saw him one more time. He was riding his motorcycle in the park.

RE: COYLE

She weighed 500 pounds at the time of her fall. Her secluded, sheltered life came to an end. The nursing home/rehabilitation facility where she stayed for a year, drained much of her resources.

To the casual or uninvolved observer, this was a tragedy. They knew nothing of her life and how she came to this.

The daughter of an overbearing Mother, the play *Night Mother* would often come to mind when thinking of their relationship.

With the help of a relative, after one long year, she got out of the home. She was able to stay in her house and rarely left the confines of her basement apartment.

She was happy during this time and spent her days reading, knitting, and watching the television, all at the same time.

No one ever knew of her dreams or aspirations. In truth, she may have never had many but on her 50th birthday, she cried all day. Her life recalls John Prime's song "Hello in There."

She had been feeling bad for a long time. A doctor's visit revealed she had stage 4 liver cancer. The end was not long in coming.

I was holding her hand when she passed. Some find all this depressing and it is. We can't all have perfect lives—do any of us?

A DAY IN THE LIFE

He had the life of a cicada or cigale en Francais. He lived in a basement apartment for 17 years. He then emerged, mated and died.

He left his shelter at 17, having few thoughts other than to procreate. Naturally, his approach was not subtle, and he questioned his lack of success.

Walking in a heavily populated grove of trees, he saw a young woman, also walking. She was alone.

As he had no real sense of societal manners, he approached her and took her in his arms. A passive woman, she did not resist his advances as he shed his clothes. But as he pressed himself upon her supine body, she struck his temple with a rock she felt lying by her side. It killed him.

The life a cicada is not so dramatic, but his life ended much as their lives did.

CEMETERY JAUNTS

Many don't understand my routine perambulations in a local cemetery. It is the only place I ever felt I belonged. Family outings on Sundays often found us there.

There are the regular graves that I visit. Little Rudy Bouvier -1900 to 1905- I question what shortened his young life as I leave a flower in remembrance. The Luoung's grave will have a receptacle in which to place the incense stick I burn. Did I know her? No. For a few years she walked the earth the same time I did. Her husband of 50 years will eventually join her there. He must find comfort in that. Another stop is to see Jean's grave that has a moon and star on it. She was a former colleague and died after giving birth to twin boys. I was glad to see that there was a wreath on her grave at Christmas. She has not been forgotten by the boys that never knew her.

Sometimes odd stares are cast in my direction as I listen to my music and walk briskly on the winding cemetery paths. Is it disrespectful to listen to music when I visit? No, these dead, they loved music, loved to sing, and dance and shared every human emotion we know.

There is the grave that says, "FELL ASLEEP." A worthy end wished for us all... to go silently in our sleep. And as a realist I know that is impossible. There is the military section or as the sign reads "the bivouac of the dead." The Gettysburg address overlooks the Civil War graves and is moving to read while gazing upon the field of soldiers.

Morbid? Maudlin? No, simply a congregation of the dead. These grounds hold no spirits, none to terrorize dreams. They exist by no longer existing.

And what do I get from these frequent perambulations? I find peace, and tranquility, inspiration and tragedy.

I Could Hear Myself Breathe

In Time
I saw the nightmare, a cruel world of chaos
and destruction.

Behold the Ephemera
Do I love flowers because they have beauty
and short lives?

Rinse
I like the anonymity of a laundromat on a
rainy day.

Laurence
I felt pain for her as I dropped the old
suitcase off at the Goodwill.

Sorry
I am not usually/always politically correct
when it comes to the subtleties of communication.

Remorse
Once I stared into the sun trying to blind
myself.

Desolate
There was the lonely hum of a single-engine
plane flying overhead.

Disillusioned
The difficulty with reality is I sometimes can't
distinguish what is real and what isn't.

Travel
The clerk at the railway station in Brussels
was the most bored person on the planet.

Originality
Follow in your own footsteps.

George
He read with relish describing the servant girl
kissing her master's feet.

Simplicity
I hope I will always be happy with what I
have.

Old
The indignity of aging.

Me
I swear that child is going straight to hell.

Question

What would it have been like to be Salvador
Dali's love?

Self-Doubt
When your own words echo mockingly in
your head.

Disillusionment Again
When you don't know the sound of your
own voice.

It's a Sin to be a Mocker
The ravens call down to me mockingly from
the tops of the trees.

Sentient
She had a characteristic face one that
reflected thoughts and laughter.

So What
You can be paranoid and believe "they" are
tapped into you someway--or just that you are in tune
with the universe and these things just play out
parallel to you.

Misplaced
When I was a child, say about six years old, I
dug a large hole in the backyard and made that my
home.
My Aunt
"It is the end of the world," she just didn't
want to think that life would go one without her.

Louie Renfro
With her red hair and stylish dress and the
Mustang she drove, she was so memorable.

John
His face is a caricature of Beavis and Butt
Head, never know one from the other.

Huh?
A tale of misguided undergarments.

Imagine
A voice in the crowd-What?

Cousin Charles
I found it disturbing that on our scenic drive,
we ended up at a crematorium.

Childhood
At nine I was standing on my head on the
couch pretending the ceiling was the floor--
mesmerized.

Dylan
Bob, the times didn't really change that
much.

Descending
Watching the sun slip downward in the sky--
peace.

Hmmm
I like to look at smiling faces; however, I
question what goes on behind those eyes.

Susan
"People say the most peculiar things to you."

Epiphany
Small minds have big mouths.

Tinnitus
In my case, not too unpleasant really, sounds like crickets on a hot summer night.

Bite Me
Teeth are wicked weapons.

Barry
"Oh yes, I remember the eyes."

Abandonment
Don't help me, don't help me, please help me.

Just a description of a colleague.
Malicious with a twisted sense of humor and an overactive imagination.

The House
I like certain angles in here and how the light can define them.

France
I often left a fingernail everywhere I stayed those three weeks of summer.

Future Shock
"Well, she has on blue shoes."

Homeless
I could live vicariously through the cat that prowls on warm fall evenings.

Destiny
When I'm gone, I want to be remembered as the one that had a twinkle in her eye.

Heathcliff
I like dark and brooding.

Substance
Being told you look great and feeling like there is nothing there.

Pastime
I am trying to become ambidextrous.

Determined
I may yet come to a bad end.

Descartes Monologue
I think therefore I am; I think I can.

Dialogue
Are you talking to me?

Perspective
The world looks different when peering through a camera lens.

Fall Pastime
Watching the trees from my kitchen window.

Listen
Have we always required entertainment?

Christmas
The shoebox filled with silver tinsel was
magical.

Warren Zevon
His left eye expressed such a world-weary
gaze.

Realization part deux
It still only hurts when I breathe.

The Neighbor
Him, with his fastidious wave and his simian
features.

Don't
Are we all prone to pre-conceived notions?

Revelation
You never know someone until you ride
passenger with them in the car.

Animated
The world is my muse.

The Professor
Him, with his sophomoric sense of humor.

Reaching
It is not that I am sweet, I am not, but I am
thoughtful.

Nancy
She had her dreams, but they were never
realized.

World Weary
A matter of oversimplification.

Devon
"I hate beautiful cats."

Driving
I love the lights reflecting on the rain swept
street.

Life
It is just a matter of dying.

Arrived at a conclusion.
A mask is my mask.

Accurate
It read that as one grows older, they are
concerned more with the conditions of the world.

Yes
And I wanted something to believe.

Deposit
Sometimes I am afraid; I want to retreat.

Exasperation
My life is so different than what people think.
But then, I don't know what they think.

Louie Again
What was she thinking as she sat there night
after night, drinking?

Ridicule
That final indignity.

Solitude
Love to be able to see the end of the day with
the setting sun.

Tried
I wasn't going to play saucy wench with him

Christmas Again
I hurt to see the T-shirt with the satin heart at
its center.

Thanks, Mother
It took me years to love or nurture.

Happy Ending
And life became more selectively perfect.

Never
Scary...power over another person.

Actual
I cultivate my eccentricities.

Jealousy
Secret envy...composer of music.

Me?
Poor mixed up kid.

Broken
As the cup tumbled to the floor, I was glad
when it shattered.

Who?
He was subject to ways of the flesh?

Well...
You don't know, you just don't know.

No Exit
I have a foolish existence.

Ruby
I was warmed by the smile of a child.

Scorched
I had forgotten about how cynical I have
become.

Katherine
I'll put forsythia in the crystal vase in the
spring.

Roosevelt
1940, it was just as bad, just fewer people.

Rollie
"Generally, that is the way a person is, there is no changing them, accept them for what they are."

Lens
As I grow older, I have developed more of a photographer's eye-observer not participator.

Frankenstein
Having a Mary Shelley moment, listening to the thunder and watching the lightning.

12-29-16
Today has been a series of misfortunate events.

Scorched again.
I want to live in a world that doesn't exist.

Me, again.
I don't get even well.

My sister
Got to look at her as interesting.

Nancy, again.
The funeral is over, and now you just go on living.

When
How to get along: be personable.

Fame
Was never famous, only infamous.

Church
Only wanted my first communion in order to
get the sweet rolls.

Perseverance
After many years, I grew a heart.

Introspection
I really was a motherless child.

Mourning
It only hurts when I breathe.

You
I didn't realize I was being regarded with such
scrutiny.

Although
Leaving behind memories like a deciduous
tree in fall.
Insight
I think I see the beauty in flowers that
Georgia O'Keefe did.

Love
Heartwarming to see how genuine children
can be.

Individual
My emotions should be opaque.

Childhood

What you grew up with is so much a part of what you are today...no revelation there.

Butterfly
Thoughts flit rapidly through my mind.

Blush
When I don't listen, it is my way of shutting someone out; is that true for most people?

The Ocean
Passing cars sound like waves on the shore.

Guilty
People love to be self-righteous.

Content
I really do live a simple life.

Scope
Why do people always have to tell you when they are scheduled for a colonoscopy?

Recognition
The shape of my head indicates that Mother never held me as an infant; my sister's head has the same shape.

Just Because
Many thoughts can be related to music, both lyrics and melody.

Huh? again
We all absorb a large amount of information and some of it sticks.

Reality
To an extent, we all exaggerate, some more than others.

Maybe
I wonder what it would be like to be all instinct.

Insight
No one truly appreciates a flower garden quite as much as the one who plants it.

Laundry
I like the whole process.

Clutch
Even when my feelings are hurt; it manages
to make me feel alive.

Pity
Was it a feral-like childhood, with neither
affection nor feeling of love?

Me
I am solitary and not particularly clever.

NBCSN
Sports can be the great equalizer in social
conversation.

Let Go
Never thought anyone could love me.

Why? again
Sometimes you just need somebody to tell
you everything will be alright.

Human
Always been afraid of what lurks deep within
us all.

Why? again
Ambiguity, one of my favorite words.

Usually
As we grow older, we begin to think about
what can go wrong.

When
The ability to empathize is not always a good
trait or an easy trait.

Doubtful
It is not as if I gave up religion, I was born a
disbeliever.

Spring
Sunlight streaming through the Dogwood
blossoms imbues a feeling of peace.

Impulsive
When one thing leads to another.

Delphine
The sadness never quite leaves her eyes.

Delight
Some watch the city as the lights begin to
appear. I watch the lights of the garden ignite!

My Mother
The poor tortured soul.

None
All I wanted was to be loved, when I was, I
didn't know what to do with it.

Feral?
Thinking back on childhood, I like to think
of myself as a little heathen.

Tune
The peaceful sound, the lulling sound, of the washing machine is a peaceful time.

Inevitable
Are there always things that one does not like about oneself?

Thoughtfulness
A glowing attribute.

Joseph
"Tu as les yeux du chat."

Rivalry
I am afraid it can be women's nature.

Time
I don't want to wish it away.

Lawrence
He liked bright and shiny.

Mammy
I only saw my great-grandmother smile once; it left an impression.

Butterfly Logic
It was a poor, pitiful fritillary.

Biology
Someone to meet in the past: one of my choices-Gregor Mendel.

Him
I want to be the one that got away.

Tally
I worshipped the gods of rock 'n roll.

Many
I have no hidden talent; I searched-nothing.

Spark
I want a fantasy, not the reality of a
relationship.

Sunday
I burned the shirt I wore that night.

Grandpapa
He called my occupation "L'etudiant de vie"-
-student of life.

Peggy
She gets lost in thoughts of the past.

Time
Most disconcerting not to remember a
sequence of events.

When again
I have bandied about verbally and have done
well when I did; I just don't do it often.

Timing
Learn to accept the things you will never
know.

Me
Yes, I was bat shit crazy.

Despite
Sometimes I don't want to join the human
race.

Faux Pas
Why do I always say "nice to see you" to
blind people?

Perplexed
It seems people rarely ask one another "what
do you mean?"

A search
I want my soul to be at rest when I die. There
are souls that aren't.

FYI
I don't have a bucket list. I don't want to die
having regret for things not done.

Pandora
I like shuffle.

Phil
"I like the way people look at you."

Cinderella Complex
I am not missing one sock, I am missing one
shoe.

Butterfly
Would love to be a butterfly in a cocoon,
come into the world beautiful, flit about a few days,
then die.

C'est la vie.
Life has been one big experiment.

Cries
Crying, really crying, is such a genuine
emotion.

Deny
Sometimes I don't want to join the human
race.
Realization
There are those that have and those that want
what they have.

What I want?
I only know what I don't want

Huh? again
And what after all does 'Cock and bull Story"
mean?

Guilty
False bravado.

Solace
I am rarely good at clever banter

Suspended
I don't like gadgets.

Doubt
Jesus never teaches you to survive.

I know
Insatiable curiosity.

Undeniable
There are parallels in life.

Often
The battle within.

Contradiction
I am an optimistic nihilist.

Remembrance
Oh, that was way out when.

Stop
I believe in arrested development.

A Quiet Mind
Because sometimes it needs to be.

My Sister
She fascinates me.

For a Song
There are just certain melodies that strike a chord in the soul.
Mind
For the most part, I am comfortable with my thoughts.

T.V.
I watch it so I won't think.

Affluence
Buy the more expensive mushrooms.

Pastis
Can you be a culinary hedonist, a pleasure
seeker of the palette?
Cats
I am going to cultivate my selective hearing.

Steve
"She will say anything."

Again
I could never be called a great
communicator.

Innuendo
Why does there always seem to be sub-text?

Demons
I have enough of them.

Me
I realized I was pretty at 13, acknowledged it,
then forgot about it.
Who?
She stirred her tea in the center of her cup,
never touching the sides.

My Dad
"Be a brave little Anglo-Saxon soldier."

Religion
There is nothing sadder than a loss of faith.

Culpability
I have been blamed for things most of my
life, rarely accused.

Spirit
It is all we have.

Insight
I am just another part of humanity.

Sometimes
I follow blindly.

Exit
Always have an escape plan.

Insanity
How much of it is my imagination?

Home Life
I am deranged.

Greatest aphorism
Happiness is a poor memory.

Shadows.
Those that can remain in the heart.

500 Miles
I travel great distances in time with music.

Dilemma
It's never too late to come to a bad end.
A Dream
If I had lived by the ocean, my life would
have been more dramatic.

A Comfort
Sometimes it is good that there are things you
will never know.

A Plea
Don't overthink everything.

Disconcerting
A Lost memory.

Blurred Daze
Sometimes glimpses of the past.

Possessed
I have never wanted someone else's
possessions, I just wanted to get through life.

The Collective Spirit
Trying to join in with the human race.

Query
If one is told they are "destructive" does that
make one self-destructive?

Demented
I hold my own, for the most part.

Strange Thoughts
My whole life is made up of them.

Yes
There is something to be said about mating
for life; however, it is less so in the human species.

Me Again
My first intelligible words spoken were "All
by myself."

Overheard Conversation.
"She doesn't talk like us."

Proust Questionnaire
When Vanity Fair asks who is your favorite
person, alive or dead, my response would be Bridget
Bardot.

Ah-Ha!
I have my memories, some not so very good.

Hockey
Boys getting aggressive with one another.

Lesson Learned
Don't make yourself do anything.

Cell Phones
You can now talk to yourself in the car and
no one would raise an eyebrow.

Yes
I can say I don't care about many things.

Childhood Memory
Wading in the creek beside Squirrel Island.

It is Spring
That is when I miss the Fall.

Loss
I never use anything to its full potential.

Yep
That is exactly when I want to stop breathing.

Pedestrian
No, it's alright; it only hurts when I breathe